# THE SCIENTIFIC THOUGHTS OF A SPIRITUAL SCIENTIST!

The scientific thought of Maharshi Mahamanas :
The great sage of the modern times

BY

MAHARSHI MAHAMANAS (Sumeru Ray)

ISBN 978-93-5438-041-9

© Maharshi MahaManas (Sumeru Ray) 2020
Published in India 2020 by Pencil

A brand of

One Point Six Technologies Pvt. Ltd.

123, Building J2, Shram Seva Premises,

Wadala Truck Terminal, Wadala (E)

Mumbai 400037, Maharashtra, INDIA

E connect@thepencilapp.com

W www.thepencilapp.com

# Author biography

Maharshi MahaManas alias

Sumeru Ray.

He is a great-minded wise sage of the modern age, a multi-talented creator, researcher, writer, philosopher, awakener, educator, multifaceted free thinker and he is self-dedicated to human development.

He is the pioneer of reasonable spirituality and the creator of the great doctrine– 'MahaVad', and the founder of 'MahaDharma' –the religion of free-thinkers for true self-development & human development.

Maharshi is well experienced physician of Alternative Medicines, he is a very successful practitioner and researcher in the field of Alternative Medicines and Human Development. MahaManas is the inventor of the new system of medicine~ MPathy…

He is a knowledge worshipper, educated in the open school of the world! Self-conscious and self-aware man of vast experience with art sense, creative power, computer knowledge, new ideas. He is a good mentor. He is an author – philosopher –researcher. Maharshi is the teacher of true self development Education 'MahaManan' and specialist in mental problems. Most important identity of MahaManas, –he is a humanitarian. His all efforts are – for human welfare. He is a social reformer.

He has knowledge in fine arts, literature, Yoga, meditation, art of healing, self-development program, lyric, story, screenplay writing, music composing and film making, news paper and periodicals editing, and reasonable spirituality.

To know more, go through Google search= Sumeru Ray / Maharshi MahaManas

# Contents


Preface.................................................07

The Time New Theory ......................................08

The Space~................................................15

What exactly Destiny is ..................................20

Time Traveling............................................24

Mind is like a blooming lotus ............................26

S-existence Another Existence.............................31

Organic Software of an Organism ..........................41

Beware of Poison Toxin....................................44

The Evidence of God-intelligence .........................46

A new system of medicine .................................48

The scientific way to alleviate global poverty ...........68

Can science be believed without hesitation ...............73

# Preface

Many people may sneeze when they hear the name of spiritual science. The spirituality of Maharishi Mahamanas is rational/ reasonable spirituality, free from superstition ~ blind-faith. This spirituality is not conventional religious spirituality.

The essence of true spirituality is to know oneself, to know this 'I'. In order to know oneself or the 'I' properly, one has to know the universe of which this 'I' is a part, that is, the cosmic order. You have to know the truth of creation, then you will be able to know the mystery of the creation of this 'I'.

The main goal of spirituality is to find the root and root cause of creation along the path of reasoning with a free mind. As you continue on this path, the cosmic mysteries will gradually unfold to you. There is no difference between science and spirituality

# The Time New Theory

**Time Oh My Time!**

by Maharshi MahaManas (Sumeru Ray)

In a word, TIME is nothing but the length of events that happen one after the other.

Just as the mind is an entity arising from the action of the brain, so is time --- a special entity arising from any form of action. Visually, a non-existent existence. S-existence (Please see separate article about it)!

If there is an action, time will be created from it. And if the action repeats itself continuously, in a certain speed and in a certain way, through a certain set of rules and regulations, then only a sensible and measurable time is created. This form can be used to measure the lifespan and action-span of other objects, individuals, etc. on the basis of that form of time.

In short, in order to facilitate the understanding of the variou parts or episodes of the act of rotating the earth or any action taking place in such a loop, the length of the event is called 'Time' by imagining an existence as a span of action.

The lifespan or age of a thing, usually from its birth to death or creation to the end or a certain part of its lifespan, refers to its duration as a measurable period arising from the regular motion of the earth. Every object, substance and organism has its own action and (even if it is in the calculation of the time of the earth or something else) it has its own time.

In practical terms, when we say 'morning-evening', we do not only refer to time, but also to a particular or a group of natural and related activities or events, environments and situations that occur in a regular cycle at that particular time.

We are accustomed to seeing time in its various episodes, in particular forms. That form is revealed to us in the form of time. But there really is no form of time. The concept of our time is born out of the changing nature and succesive stream of events.

It is said, time imprint, time power, time gift etc. As if time has its own power or ability by which it can do many things. In reality there is no independent form of time, no quality. In a series of endless activities or events, one action after another or events are happening. One by one, a special form, a special loss or gain occurs in one of the episodes of the sequence of events that take place gradually through different interactions.

We measure them in time, bringing the sequence of events into our imagination. We say that what have to be happen will happen at the right time. We say, when the time comes, it will happen .... etc. But that doesn't mean that time will tell. The fact that time is a powerful entity has not yet been proven.

In this context, I say that destiny, like time, is a seemingly non-existent special existence arising from action. As soon as creation begins, they, that is, both worldly time and destiny, come into existence.

How fast are we? In addition to our activities and mobility, we are under the motion of the earth. We are connected with the motion of the solar system, not just the earth. Again, we are moving at unimaginable speeds through the entire cosmic motion, including our nebula.

Any object or creature with high activity or speed, compared to a similar object or creature with low activity or slow motion, if there is no irregularity or mishap, will accomplish its specific task long ago, will reach the goal, will have consequences, will be eroded, will age And will run out or attain fusion. That means its/his lifespan will be much shorter than the other, due to its/his rapid aging based on his own time.

However, if an organism or a person with a long life is highly active, it will not age rapidly unless it is afflicted with a disease, if it lacks the necessary food and drink, and if no non-occurrence occurs.

However, conventional scientific sources say that if the activity or speed of an object or person is the fastest--- approaching the speed of light, then its time will continue to be very slow. As a result, its age will continue to grow very slowly. Unless an accident occurs, its lifespan or longevity will be many times longer than that of a similar object or person with normal motion. However, if an object gains the same speed as the speed of light, then it will no longer exist as an object or a person.

As we have seen in my cosmology, everything has become fixed from the beginning. Where will it happen, when will it happen. With the beginning of creation, the cycle of the universe has begun.

As soon as you are born, the clock of your time starts ticking. Once a device is made, it is determined (depending on the environmental conditions and its components) how long it will serve and how long it will survive with its uniqueness. The same is true of our body organs.

Is time just a psychological or conceptual existence of man, or is it a reality! Whether one realizes it or not, time exists in its own existence. Rather sometimes people's perceptions about time can be misleading. Sometimes a short time can seem like a lot of time to someone. Again, the opposite can happen.

If an object or thing is slow or fast, it may take a long time or a short time to get from one (event) position to another (event) position (depending on the measurable time generated from another event that is constantly moving).

That active or moving object has its own time but depends on its activity or speed. There, if it's/ his speed slows down, it's/ his time will also slow down. If it's/ his speed is fast, it's/ his time will also be fast. There will be no exceptions or vice versa. That is, if its/ his speed is fast, its/ his time will not slow down.

There are two types of relativity. The first is comparative judgment between multiple subjects. And the second is the comparative judgment of something with its own in different situations.

The relativity I am referring to here is the relativity of something to itself. Here it is being compared with something of high speed and its relatively low speed.

Slowing down in time means getting longer. Generally, if one's speed is faster than before, then the speed of one's time will also be faster than before. And as a result, his lifespan will be reduced. As the speed or activity of an object increases, its lifespan will decrease due to more erosion.

However, according to Einstein, if something moves faster than before, its time will decrease and its lifespan will increase. Now the question is, if his own speed does not slow down, how does his (own) time slow down!

If an object or something is slow or fast, it may take a long time or a short time to move from one (event) state to another (event) state (depending on the measurable time generated from another regularly moving event).

That moving object has its own time but depends on its speed. There, if its speed slows down, its time will also slow down. If irs speed is fast then its time will also be fast. There will be no exceptions or vice versa. That is, if its speed is fast, its time will not be slow.

If no external force is applied on a moving object, the 'Time' generated by the motion of the object will remain normal. Its time will not slow down.

If an object is moving in space (although not actually zero), its loss will be less or not. Its lifespan will be almost the same, or its lifespan will not be much shorter. This is the general idea.

But if the object moves very fast, its attraction power will be greater, its 'gravity' will be higher. As a result, lots of cosmic particles will jump on it. And then its speed will be hindered and its condition will change.

That high-velocity object will gradually fill up with cosmic particles. That is, the amount of cosmic particles in it will continue to increase and the normal state of the object will continue to change gradually.

As a result, the lifespan of the object will gradually decrease. And the shorter the lifespan, the faster the time. Its time will soon run out.

According to conventional theory, the higher the gravity of an object, the slower its own time will be. But if the object does not have a self-defense mechanism, if it cannot protect itself from cosmic energy or particles, then its lifespan will be reduced. And, shortening its lifespan means speeding up its (own) 'Time'.

In this context, even in the case of the highest dynamic light, its 'time' is created. It takes a lot of time to come to Earth from a distant galaxy. Therefore, it cannot be said that its 'Time' has slowed down due to the highest speed.

Time, space and destiny were created at the same time as the creation of the universe through the Big Bang. Although these virtual entities are interdependent and interconnected, they have distinct entities.

In the end, the virtual entity called 'Time' has come into existence with the creation of the universe. As soon as the universe reaches its end, the existence of 'Time' will also be destroyed.

# The Space~


The Space~ Time and Destiny (New theory)
by Maharshi MahaManas (Sumeru Ray)

All over the univers--- a bubble like multidimensional, seemingly unobstructed or nearly unobstructed vacuum existence is called space.

This space existence came into being as the universe was created through the great explosion. And as the universe progresses, this space is gradually expanding.

This space is actually a special existence composed of invisible unperceived--- extraordinary particles of a particular frequency. These particles, like 'Stem cell', themselves grow at a rapid rate when needed. Science has not yet been able to discover them.

In general, this space is an invisible unfelt non-existent existence to us. That is why it is called a great vacuum.

Therefore, this space is not absolute zero. Absolute zero lies outside the universe. In which the great creation and the universe inhabits.

Our space is not empty at all. In addition to its own existence, it is filled with various cosmic rays --- energy, particles and radiation. It does not usually participate in various activities, including action-reaction, attraction and repulsion between those forces and particles. It is neutral--- idle indifferent.

Not only that everything in the universe is inhabited by space, also there is space inside everything. In fact, space does not contain anything --- neither does exclusion. It is like its own.

As the universe was created--- in addition to space, two more indivisible unique virtual existences were created. That is 'Time' and 'Destiny' (please see 'Time' and 'Destiny' essay note). Some blend space and time together. But time and space are two distinct entities. The great relationship between time and space is that they are born from the same phenomenon.

Just like fish inside aquatic waters, so is our position in this space. There is space inside and outside--- on all sides of us.

Some have described this unique space as different in their imagination. But none of them are the true form of this mysterious space. The space still remains intangible to us.

In this context, a small piece of a 'Bangla' poem I wrote at a young age was remembered!

'How is this space!?
Frequently the same question---
Then I look for a while
With zero vision.
Can't find anything---
How do I get it!
There is still a long way to go.
The chariot of creation
Is still in the dark.
It gropes the answer of
Self-inquiry. As a part,
That question is raised repeatedly inside me.'

To understand the space, one has to move forward from root--- step by step. The original being is situated in absolute zero. And within it the space with the universe was born (see my latest cosmogony blog). At the beginning of my cosmogony, there is a brief description of the absolute zero. The description is as follows:

Absolute zero! The rootless endless formless actual zero. Not our known space. Beyond the area of the universe, beyond the territory of the original being--- The everlasting vacuum that exists --- that absolute zero!

Silent --- waveless--- indifferent---
a non-existent existence. Within that unchanged--- indestructible--- steadfast zero, unable to access any moving material or energy from here.

The original being is situated in that absolute zero. And the great creation was born in that original being. This great creation is made up of a large number of universes. One of them is our universe.

In my cosmogony, there is a description of the original being as follows:

Original being lies at a certain limit in the middle of that absolute zero. The original being is mainly composed of the original particles--- the absolute particles, and the original energies. It is also full of numerous joint particles and radiation, with the absolute conscious-mind (in philosophy).

The pre-great-creation like a fruit made up of many universe seeds is created through first explosion. And, at one time, there was a great explosion in the universe-seeds of this fruit like pre-superstructure. From which sprouted up--- the universes are evolving like countless trees.

Different elemental particles and energies with different frequencies are created from original particle's different levels of vibration. There are different type of programming codes (nearly similar to the computer programming code) at the core of the component of original particles and elementary particles.

It is important to mention here that the original particle has no 'dimension'. The original particle is a virtual entity, created by that type of programming code or at the root of which is the special programming code.

Different particles of different frequencies created from the original particles are actually the embodiment of the latent programming code.

Eventually, when this cosmic collapse will take place, as soon as the space is destroyed.

My theory about space is ~
This gradually expanding seemingly empty space is not empty at all. Space is an incomparable existence, made of inexperienced special particles of a particular frequency. Particles that are capable of growing themselves by the birth of new particles, such as the cell division process. Let's name these space particles--- 'MahaManas' particles.

# What exactly Destiny is

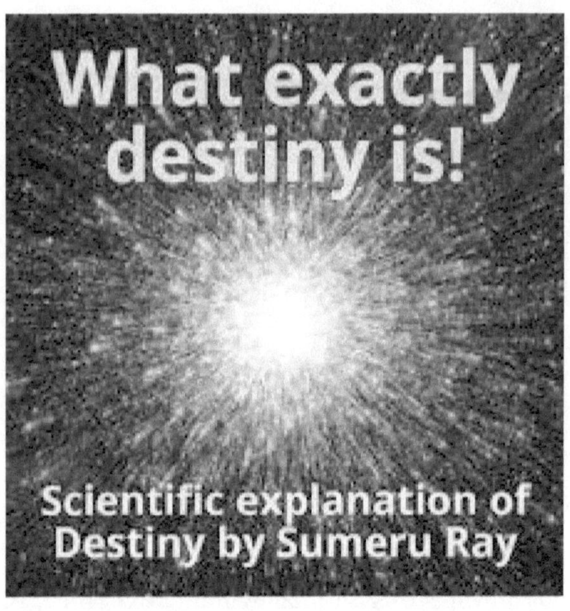


**What exactly Destiny is!**
**~Maharshi MahaManas (Sumeru Ray)**

Destiny : From the view-point of science
(Scientific explanation of Destiny)

~Sumeru Ray (Maharshi MahaManas)

The destiny (luck/fortune/fate) is a self-made automatic (worldly) system which came into existence with the creation of the universe through the great explosion (Big Bang).

In this system, it is automatically determined at the moment of the explosion --- when and where --- what would happen in the traditional event. Its name is Destiny.

Whatever is happening here, Destiny is at the root of everything, Destiny is responsible for everything. This Destiny is predetermined and unchanging.

However, Destiny has to move forward along the path of logic based on a variety of factors, in order to be effective.

Some of us are happy, some are sad, some are successful, and some are unsuccessful because of Destiny. We suffer so much for our Destiny. Therefore, Destiny needs to know very well.

In fact, Destiny is a self-made system created by an event, which is depending on the space-time, situation-environment, becomes effective through the causation-reasoning, action-reaction of traditional events, and inevitably determines future events.

In the cosmic field: Destiny is a kind of involuntary force or self-created program, that arise at the beginning of the creation of the world through the beginning of the Great Explosion! And it is the determinant and regulator of the inevitable future events.

Each produced event is the apparent cause of the various events that occur in the future in connection with its which is automatically predetermined at the beginning of the creation of the universe.

For ease of understanding, let's say with a simple pattern: The rotation of the rotating wheel with an arrow blade is determined automatically as soon as it starts, when and where the sharp angle of the arrow blade will go. This is Destiny and predetermined event. It is almost the same as in the case of Great Creation or worldly events. Its fate has been determined automatically at the beginning of creation.

Destiny is active in different ways, inside and outside of us, knowingly and unknowingly. All our activities, including our thoughts, desires are contribution of Destiny or fate, and are part of the worldly activities.

We are also a part of this world. Here, fortunately or incidentally some are rich --- some are poor, some are noble and some are dishonest. That is to say, there is no controller or determinant and controlling entity behind it, there is a self-created automatic mechanical system.

Creation begins with the Great Explosion, and in that instant the Destiny is born (That's how TIME is born). Actually Destiny is a virtual existence. For example, an explosion of a bomb occurs after a series of incidents. The explosion is automatically determined by the moment, what happens next, and then, traditionally, after each other. Everything that is happening in this world and everything that will happen, determined --- almost automatically at the moment of the Great Explosion!

Multiple events are born from one event. Again, many more events are taking place after that one. Thus the successive stream of events continues. In the present scenario, various events arising from an event cannot be followed in a definite way. External or other events created outside, objects, energies, etc., that will disrupt or affect its or their movement, or alter the course of events.

So, the examples mentioned here are just examples. These examples will not have much resemblance to the main event I discussed. The main point being discussed is the great explosion at the beginning of the universe's creation! Which is known as the Big Bang. In this case, no external object, force or event is missing to affect the original event and the numerous events that have arisen from it. Here the course of events is proceeding in a self-determined way.

# Time Traveling

Some talk in the context of 'Time Travelling'
~Maharshi MahaManas (Sumeru Ray)

You are nothing but a short-lived character in this gigantic cosmic film, consisting of one frame after another.

In this movie, as a character in a mega serial drama, it is not possible for you to go to the past or the future of this movie.

So, 'Time travel' is an unrealistic fantasy. Surprisingly, some people see science in this fantasy! Also there are many scientists among them !!

They also continue to call various hypotheses about time as science. In reality, time is nothing but the length of events that happen one after the other.

Everything that is happening in the universe, including the multi-universe, is predetermined (Please see my article about 'Destiny'). Just like a film or a video.

As it's possible to watch a video by moving forward or backward, it may even be possible for a viewer outside the cosmos to watch the video of this cosmic-event-stream by moving forward or backward.

Because of that, neither you nor I, as a character in this video, can forward or backward the video as a viewer outside the video. So, 'Time Travelling' is an unrealistic idea.

# Mind is like a blooming lotus

Mind is like a blooming lotus
~Maharshi MahaManas (Sumeru Ray)

Mind is our main topic. Here, who (or which) is saying is Mind, and you, who (or which) is listening is also Mind. The principal creator and driver of our world, and also of the cosmos –is Mind. A little and sweet name– Mind! In this world, whatever we are seeing – whatever is happening, whatever has been created and is creating, behind all creation– there is Mind. Only creatures have Mind, –not that, there is a cosmic mind. The Mind of highest conscious level!

We are human beings, because we have wakeful– conscious Mind. All other creatures have also Mind, but their Minds are different lower conscious level's Minds. They have not (human) conscious Mind.

Mind is like a computer-OS-software, with many active and inactive application softwares. Whole body with brain– with nervous system and sense organs –is like computer-hardware. At present, in our mental world, there we have two active partner Minds. One is pre-human conscious Mind or sub-conscious Mind, and another is conscious Mind or human conscious Mind.

In our mental world, this sub-conscious Mind is most bloomed or developed, and active. Now it is engaged in work in the main role. It has some special qualities. If we can utilize them properly, in many cases, we can be benefited and can achieve success. But this Mind has some bad qualities, for that, we need to control this Mind.

In case of greater number human beings, gradually developing or blooming (human) conscious Mind –till now, is a little developed (bloomed) and a little active. In case of human beings, it has an important role. We have (human) conscious Mind; this is why we are human beings. Still it is not enough developed. We need to develop our Mind, to be enough developed human beings.

Two Minds are living together as like as spouse, reasonable (human) conscious Mind (The Mind of male nature) as a husband, and blind-emotional sub-conscious Mind ( The Mind of female nature) as a wife. Depending on their characters, I think, they are similar to Hindu Goddess 'Kali' and lord 'Shiva' –largely. Remember the picture of 'Kali' and 'Shiva' where 'Shiva' is about sleeping under the foot of 'Kali'!

In appearance a human being –female or male, however be s/he, female and male (more or less) both natures are present there. As much as conscious Mind is developed in a human being, so much manly human is s/he. On the other hand, as less as conscious Mind is developed in a human being, so much womanly human is s/he.

As much as our conscious Mind will be developed, so much we will be developed human beings. In the aim of fully developed human beings, to cause to occur the development of conscious Mind –is our inherent aim of life. By this conscious Mind –consciously, we have to utilize the subconscious Mind, for its good qualities, and we have to control it for its bad qualities.

But most of human beings are not aware about their Mind, due to lack of enough development –enough consciousness. Regarding human development –development of our country and society, we have seen many endeavors, but in the root of all development, there is Mind. We have no endeavor for true development of our Mind.

Spirit or 'Atma' means inner self, which is Mind. Whether it human bodied or not, human Mind or higher conscious Mind, or God Mind, a conscious existence which can feel –can think –is Mind.

Whole Mind is like a blooming lotus. Our present active Minds (conscious and sub-conscious Minds) are not whole Mind. Whole Mind is somewhat like a blooming lotus. There are many parts or partner Minds, and many state or stages of mental development. Whole Mind is formed by many active and inactive Minds.

Entire Mind is like a blooming lotus –largely. Lotus like whole Mind –containing various partner Minds of different conscious level, through different blooming state or stages, – according to serial order of development, step by step –(one after one Mind) blooms gradually.

From latent conscious state, gradually worm or insect conscious Mind, and then reptile conscious Mind blooms one after one. At the next step or stage of blooming petals of lotus like Mind, animal conscious Mind is opened there. After that, previous-human (sub) conscious Mind blooms gradually. And in next turn, human conscious petals (Mind) open slowly. Gradually, Deva (super human) conscious Mind, after that, MahaDeva (great) conscious Mind opens little by little. In this way– all petals bloom one by one. The goal is full-consciousness. To make understand, here I have described a few mentionable steps and forms of Minds. In this lotus like Mind, there are many more mental state and different level of conscious Minds.

The last serial order of blooming consciousness is God-conscious Mind or God-Mind. Even though, there is an ultimate state of lotus-Mind, when all petals will be bloomed and when all petals will fall down, then the remaining part with seed –is the original conscious Mind. That is 'Paramatma.' From that seed re-creation will be taken place.

Those who are conscious about their own Mind, with inner world also conscious about outer world, and conscious about the cosmic Mind (Viswa-Atma), they are in fact enough conscious human beings.

# S-existence Another Existence

S-Existence and its Contrary Existence
~Sumeru Ray (Maharshi MahaManas)


Abstract:

'S-Existence' is another existence of all beings. Lack of appropriate word has caused to mark or name this unearthly existence– 'Sumeru-Existence', briefly– 'S-Existence'. This 'S-Existence' identity is too much subtle –unperceived – unfelt.

From fundamental particle to every element, – matter and energy have two different existences in its form. The formations of matter or element, components, quality, energy etc all are present in its 'S-Existence'. Generally, this 'S-Existence' is inseparable mixed with material existence.

Keywords:

S-Existence, other existence, contrary existence, Sumeru-Existence, Theoretical Physics

## S-Existence and its Contrary Existence

'S-Existence' is another existence of all beings. Lack of appropriate word has caused to mark or name this unearthly existence– 'S-Existence'. This 'S-Existence' identity is too much subtle –unperceived –unfelt.

From fundamental particle to every element, – matter and energy have two different existences in its form. The formations of matter or element, components, quality, energy etc all are present in its 'S-Existence'. Generally, this 'S-Existence' is inseparable mixed with material existence.

In case of living body it is same; it also has 'S-Existence' –unearthly body or supernatural body. 'S-Existence' of mind, – vital energy and sense etc are also present in the supernatural body.

With matter and energy, their 'S-Existence' is also mixed inseparably. With support of material body or matter, mixed with it– its 'S-Existence' is present. Without 'S-Existence' any matter– anything cannot be there. If there is change in matter or body's shape –quality, similar change takes place in its 'S-Existence'. This supernatural body or matter is a true copy of material body or matter, which is not a known matter –is an unknown and different matter –is made of unearthly matter.

When there is an action and reaction between a matter and other matter, then there takes place similar action and reaction and change between their 'S-Existence'. When a matter comes into contact with its antimatter, –both the matters as soon as the union of their 'S-Existences' –both loses their independent existence. As a result of this union, can occur the dispersion of energy, and can be created different kinds of particles, new matters –elements and energy –depending on the condition and velocity of the union.

When any matter or particle of matter has repeated collisions with other matter or matter-particle, then their S-Existences will put a contrary impression* on each other's 'S-Existence'. Everyone's 'S-Existence' will carry the contrary impression of other 'S-Existence', till the time– the carrier matter or matter-particle and along with their S-Existence's disorder– deformity or change takes place.

--------------------------------------------------------------------------------

* This contrary impression is not like two dimensional stamp-print or reverse-print. This contrary impression is a thorough –three (or more) dimensional impression of super (natural)

existence which is externally inactive and just opposite impression existence of 'S-Existence' of any material thing.

From that contrary impression of 'S-Existence' (CISE) which is a burden to the matter's 'S-Existence', many more copy of that can be produced, –then only if repeated collisions takes place with the matter or element-particle carrying that impression and similar or other matters or element particles. But in this case, contrary impression of that impression of 'S-Existence' will not be made. Depending on other matter's 'S-Existence', this contrary impression of 'S-Existence' (CISE) is merely a (material or supernatural) bodiless impression. As it is not having its own body, it is unable to impress any contrary impression on others. As a result of collisions, from that– many similar copies can be made, but gradually those copies will get more and more fineness or subtlety. From one particle to other particle, from that to other –if in this way gradually that copy is made, then gradually the copy of 'CISE' will become finer to finest.

Usually this 'CISE' is inactive –quality less. But anyhow if this 'CISE' enters the living body, then by the help of the software of bio-system, is able to get a supernatural body.

The 'CISE' on entering the living body, reaches the particular center of brain with help of nervous system. There with the special work capability of the software of bio-system, that copy of impression (CISE) gets the supernatural body. That is to say, 'CISE' turns into contrary super (natural) body or existence. Then it is not merely inactive impression, an active supernatural (body or matter) existence –endowed with quality and character –properties. The birth that it took from matter or element as 'CISE', and then it becomes contrary S-Existence of that matter or element.

Then, that contrary S-Existences spread through the circulatory system and nervous system– throughout the creature's whole body –similar to defense force. In search of enemy– culprit or evildoer those who are causes of diseases, –thoroughly searching the whole body, meeting its contrary existence –immediately it jumps on that. As a result, disappear the identity of both.

The subject is absolutely new, so let's repeat in short, – when the CISEs come into contact with the body's nervous system, –in electrical speed, they reach a particular center of the brain. There, with the help of bio-system's software, the CISEs get supernatural bodies or 'S-Existence' –according to their quality –nature –property, everyone. From there, following the defense system of the living body, –they spread out the sickly parts of the body or throughout the body –in search of alike-contrary thing which are poisonous –harmful for body.

If the nervous system and the software of the body is weak, undisciplined or incapable, that 'CISE' may not be able to get a super (natural) body or existence and not be able to follow its working role properly.

After entering of 'CISE' (of anything) in the body, if that 'CISE' converts to 'S-Existence' with the help of body-mechanism and if that 'S-Existence' does not meet the contrary existence in the body, –in that case if the number of S-Existences are too many, then they are the contrary existence of which matter or element, who were able to create as like action of poisoning in the body, these (contrary) S-Existences are able to create contrary or opposite symptom of poisoning of that thing. For example, if main thing or matter is able to create constipation, then its contrary 'S-Existence' (about which is discussing) will create diarrhea.

But if these S-Existences' number or amount is less in poisonous limit, then they will do similar activity, but it will be not so acute –not be unhealthy. Rather relieving constipation –will help to clear the bowels. That will work like mild purgative.

This action will not be stable. The cause which created the constipation, that cause will not be stopped in this case.

If the number of (contrary) 'S-Existence' is too low, then any action may not be felt. Except it, cause behind the constipation (or other incident) if there is present any strong reason or poison, in that case, the 'CSE' may not be successful in its work. But if this 'CSE' comes in contact with a thing which is similar in every respect (form –quality –character etc) in the body, then action of poisoning can be created depending on their number or amount.

In the body, when 'CSE's are able to do their own work, at the end of work –end their longevity. But those who do not get the opportunity of work, they slowly go out from the body through different paths or outlets. But everyone has its own life period.

Matter is material form of its 'S-Existence'. Any matter can never be without its 'S-Existence'. In case of energy, it is same. But the 'S-Existence' in some cases, without its material form, that is without the material body– able to remain, depending on some unearthly things. If any 'S-Existence' meets with its (exact) contrary 'S-Existence', the identity of both disappears. Along with that, if they have the material identity or existence, that also destroys.

Just like its material body, this 'S-Existence' is made by combination of quality-full unearthly particles. Atom and its inner energies and particles, fundamental particle and all other particles have 'S-Existence'. Every particle of matter or element has the similar 'S-Existence' –present in it.

The 'CISE' that entering the body– after getting the similar 'S-Existence', connecting with the harmful contrary existence, –both disappeared and destroyed. –This is the principle of 'MahaPathy' medicine's recovery procedure. I shall make an acquaintance with 'MahaPathy' next time. MahaPathy (brlefly MPathy) –the super excellent system of medicine came into existence based on this theory.

If repeated collisions takes place between two molecules or particles of similar nature and quality –for some times, –does not produce contrary impression on each others 'S-Existence'. No particle accepts its contrary impression – does not accept its contrary impression on it. Here we have to keep in mind, (contrary) impression of 'S-Existence' (CISE) and 'S-Existence' –not same.

Now what will happen, if bodily enemy or poisonous matter or anything causing the action of poisoning –instead of being exact contrary of medicine if it is partly contrary –then?

–Contrary 'S-Existence' (CSE) in medicine form (produced from CISE), after searching in the body, if does not meet its exact contrary existence, meets any partly (largely) contrary existence, then also it jumps to get united –in extreme attraction of union. In that case– depending on both's energy, amount, quality and strength along with body's condition of that time, can cause various incidents. Can occur partly alleviation or partly cure. If capable, the rest of part– body can manage oneself. Result of union can create– new matters –particles, and dispersion of rays can take place at different levels.

Except it, if any harmful poisonous germ is present in body and be attacked by that medicine, then it, for the self-defence, can assume very violent angry-looking, and can create indiscipline in bodily system. Or by escaping, can go exterior portion of the body like skin eruption. Or can try to self-hide, just like the snail.

Another thing is, if contrary impression (CISE) of any matter or element is applied repeatedly on any sensitive person, in that case, action of poisoning can take place and symptom of that poisoning can be seen. Those (medicine form) CISEs after becoming 'S-Existence' in the person's body, if they do not meet the contrary impression or contrary 'S-Existence', then also they (because of their majority) can create action of poisoning by themselves.

After any poison enters the body, medicine (CISE) prepared from that poison, at many times– is incapable of making that poison inactive. One of reasons of this is– many times, after any poison enters the body, connecting with other poisons or things present in the body, –that poison takes different form. For this reason, same poison takes different form in different bodies. As a result, the medicines (CISE) created from that poison is incapable of making inactive –the same poison. Then that has to be made inactive by any other medicine.

But anyhow, if the (mixed or unmixed) poison, is collected from body, and medicine (CISE) is made from that, –if that medicine is entered into the body, then that poison becomes inactive.

Except that, any poison, after entering the body, gradually changes take place in its form –quality –nature etc with the passing of time. The contrary 'S-Existence' of that changed condition's poison can make this changed poison– appropriately inactive (within the body).

The noticeable thing is– due to eating some amount of calcium –along with other symptoms, the secretion of bile from gall bladder will increase and with it– the temperature of the body will increase. But the medicine (CISE) prepared from that calcium, as a result of eating a lot of that medicine repeatedly, –the symptoms appeared in the body, that is opposite (symptoms) to material calcium. How it happens?

The happening is–, in the body, the particles of contrary 'S-Existence' (CSE) of calcium destroy the equal amount of calcium particles of the body. As a result, deficiency of calcium takes place, in the body. The contrary S-Existences (in a large amount) of calcium particles– create that kind of action of poisoning– in the body that is just opposite symptom of material calcium.

If that CSEs are not able to meet with similar or almost similar minute– contrary existence (matter or element), in the body, or remain some quantity –after meeting with contrary existence, then they create action or action of poisoning of different degrees –depending on their existing amount in the body.

If there is present –from before, any matter or element – endowed with similar action of poisoning, –that is to say, if similar action of poisoning is all ready present in the body, in that case, by their united action of poisoning– intense action of poisoning takes place –in the body. In such a condition, to remedy this intense action of poisoning, the defense system of the body– creates more quantity of antidotes or antitoxins. As a result of that, the poison produced from medicine, along with former poison –both are destroyed or disappeared. Besides, as medicine form 'CSE' has no material body, –the span of its life is finished in a short time.

# Organic Software of an Organism

Organic Software of an Organism

~Sumeru Ray (Maharshi MahaManas)

We know mind is amazing organic software. Besides our mind-software, there is a basic-software in every cell of an organism. And, a universal-basic-organic-software (UBOS) is present in the body of an organism which is formed by these basic software(s) unitedly. This 'UBO' software plays the fundamental and major role in conducting the organic system, and mind-software executes the remaining – outstanding works.

Basic-software and 'UBO' software work according to the 'program' –staying into the cells of the body of an organism, and mind-software works on the base of UBO software.

One part of this 'program' is recorded in a code form into the chromosome, and other part of the 'program' is recorded into the software– as like as a software program. One part is received hereditarily, and other part is earned through life-long activities.

In every organism, there is an inbuilt bio-data-card like mobile SIM card. To recognize –to control each organism individually, worldly-system arranged a code for each, in this bio-data-card. This card is always active in an organism by the help of its organic-software. It is a medium of communication with worldly-system and the system of an organism.

Every cell does its various works by its own organic software, for instance: enduring the fixed span of its life, taking food– passing stool, nutrition, remaining in sound health, keeping up its succession, keeping up mutual relation and activities with other cells, and so on.

Except these, wear and tear originating from an injury and different causes, encountering with enemies like microbes –bacilli etc., and toxins –poisons, and so on works are executed by its own organic software.

Moreover, a cell's software also works according to the order of central software of its body. Sometimes it works according to the order of the mind-software, too.

All organisms are under control of the necessity of worldly-system and its stream of events. Within that, in course of events, bad and good influences –come from surroundings– circumstances, different living beings and from other sources, are recorded as 'program' as virus in these organic software(s). These (bad and good) influences also control organism's life –largely.

In near future, these programs of organic software(s) can be deleted and/or changed according to our need. And, re-programming the organic-software can be possible then. Then, we will be able to change our life according to our need.

Even though, at present, it is possible to delete some bad and harmful 'programs' from our mind-software, by the help of Hypnotism and other methods. Also we can install any good 'program' into our mind-software by this way. In near future, there are many possibilities in the field of organic-software.

# Beware of Poison Toxin

Beware of Poison / Toxin

Now that which we are eating, water which we are drinking, air we are breathing in, all are more or less poisoned.

Every day in this way we are become poisonous. Now it is difficult to understand that who is ill and who is healthy. Doctors those who are treating us, also they are not free from poison. Knowingly or unknowingly– day after day gradually we are becoming attacked by severe diseases due to poison/toxin. Treatments are becoming impracticable.

So many poisons are there to destroy mankind. Besides deadly insecticides and bacterial poisons (toxins), many more poisons are active to make us poisonous. Influence of many electromagnetic fields and radiations are able to effect poisoning. Daily used utensils, especially cooking utensils are cause of slow poisoning (metal poisoning). Poisoning is being occurred regularly by different kind of chemicals. Food those are genetically modified, create a fatal action of poisoning in our body.

Besides these, in many places hormone is being used to increase the production of fruit and vegetable, fish, milk, chicken etc... Food and drinks those which are containing hormone, creates harmful action of poisoning in our body and mind.

Above all, the mental pollution and mental poisons are making our life more bitter and unbearable. Are you informed about internal secretion of poisons? It occurs due to mental pain, excitement and mental pollution. Except this, intemperance– irregularity is other causes of it.

If there will not happen any sudden accident, the poison/ toxin will be the cause of destruction of mankind.

# The Evidence of God-intelligence

The Evidence of God-intelligence, and Blooming of Consciousness of God (Creator})!

The trick of increasing creature's race– compelling to sexual union by allurement of sexual enjoyment and sexual urging, –is indicative of intelligence of God or The Universe-System. And it is also an evidence of presence of God mind or The Universe-Mind!

Moreover, it will be seen after minute observation, gradually to make us (from scanty-conscious human beings) more and more knowledgeable and conscious, God or the Universe System had created many nice tricks!

Besides that, gradually higher to higher creation of creatures– during billions years– little by little, is the evidence of gradual blooming of consciousness with increasing of knowledge and experience of God or the universe-mind. In this context I would like to say, the universe Existence is the real God, and there is a Universe-Mind in this body, that is God-mind!

I think the great universe is the body of God, there is also a mind in this body that is God mind. The great universe and its mind unitedly –the God existence!

The Universe is not created by God, itself God. In this universe, here is nothing except God. Only some parts of the universe, like creatures are made by God. Though, God had made these creatures by its own body-materials. Our minds are also made from universe-mind. Nothing is creatable from nothing. We all are parts of God/universe.

# A new system of medicine

MahaPathy: The super-excellent system of medicine for universal treatment

('MahaPathy' –this new system of medicine is mentioned briefly as 'MPathy')

~Sumeru Ray (Maharshi MahaManas)

The fundamental words:

Different types of disorders and/or deformities –sick conditions of different characteristic groups of cells of different parts of living body are expressed to us in form of different type of diseases or symptoms of diseases.

Here, 'disorder' is –the exception of the cell's normal action (functional disorder) or indiscipline. And 'deformity' is –the change of normal structure of cell –change of constituent parts of body-cell.

Poison is the cause of all these disorders –deformities. 'Poison' ward is used here for extensive types of meaning. Poison is that –which is capable of causing disorder – deformity in body cell. Here harmful Viruses and bacteria are also considered as poison or toxin. Different types of poisons in different amount, depending on the condition of living body, cause different disorders and /or deformities. Again, the same (in reduced amount) quantity of any poison, in case of all and in case of same creature, cannot cause same action of poisoning, all the time.

In case of creating –the action of poisoning by any poison, depending on the condition of living body, at different times, and in case of different living body, the minimum intruding (entrance) quantity of poison is not same.

But almost all things in great quantity –of this material and energy world, –are like poison to the creature. Action of poisoning may take place in the living body, by excessive use or intruding (entrance) of almost all energies – matters. Those which are not classified generally under poison list, –they also act like poison at different high quantity, in the living body.

That, which is generally very delicious or nutritious food or without which, even a moment, cannot be lived, by the creature, –that same in excess amount, grows as deadly poison for the creature. Generally in small quantity, whatever acts like poison, we all think those, to be poison. Besides different form of harmful energies –elements or matters, besides plant oriented or chemical poisons, we are being much harmed or diseased by mental poison. Besides these, as a result of excessive hard work, torture, hurt, intemperance in eating, mental pollution etc, action of poisoning may take place in the body.

Some of these disorders –deformities of cells are acquired by us (consciously or unconsciously), and some we inherit from heredity, –actually which was acquired by our ancestors. Habitually, as per capability of the body, it is always trying to make inactive, all these harmful poisonous substance. Along with that, there is arrangement, of replacement of destruction caused. Body's preventive system –defense system against the poison, –if successful in this case –the body recovers (cured) and if fails, the body gets sick.

Within the body cells, different levels of excitement, irritation or inflammation takes place, when comes in contact with different quantity of different types of poisons. As per the capability of body's preventive –defense system, it promptly gets ready, for its eradication. As a result of irregularity, torture, if excessive or abnormal loss or destruction takes place of the very necessary elements or matters of the body, then also sickness is seen. Moreover, the cause behind loss or destruction may be the sickness. If any constituent part of body is lost –generally the rest of the parts gets excess. Action of poisoning may be created, from this excess. Again, the vacuum and weakness created as a result of loss, from that, –excess of air is created in the body. Also excess of air creates the action of poisoning –unhealthiness.

Similarly, because of much sunlight– heat or taking food enriched with protein or calcium, in much quantity, more bile secretion takes place. Action of poisoning may take place in the body, from this excess of bile. Again, this excess of bile –behind this also, may be sickness. From action of poisoning loss and excess both take place. Also action of poisoning may be created from loss and excess.

Moreover, such some things (matter, element or energy) are there, any special type of action of poisoning is not seen of those in material form or gross quantity. But in subtle form or in subtle 'CISE' or 'CSE' (discussing later on) –they act or cause action of poisoning.

Some poisons are of strong active power, among these, many poisons lose their working capacity in short time, these are short acting poisons. And some poisons are long acting; – these act in slow speed, for long time. Some poisons cause the permanent deformity of body cells, of the creature, and act hereditarily generation after generation.

Every day, in the living body, birth– death of many cells continues. Immediately after the death of sick cells, if the body would have been free from its sickness, then no problem would have been there. Many sick cells –giving birth to many sick cells before their death, –then only they depart. As a result, sick cells maintain their sickly continuity –hereditarily, generation after generation. Dead cells after flowing with the blood –goes out from the body, through the urine, according to arrangement of the body-system. Not only dead cells, in the defense system of living body, – disease preventive and remedial Bio-chemicals, which have been defeated after fighting against poison or won, have been able in the remedy of sickness, of the body cells or unable, that deformed bio-chemicals also along with the urine of the creatures, go out from the living body in accordance with the body-system.

Besides this, through the urine– is passed out some parts of the destructive poison –which the body system is able to throw out from the body. And some more parts –which the body system is able to make inactive and deformed. Also some parts of sick cells are there, there are cell stool and surplus and excreted (given out) cell food Etc.

Now, if we are able to, anyhow make inactive –reduce, the different intruding poisons in the body, if we are able to make return the deformed cells to the normal condition, if we are able to make the body defense-system active– powerful – refreshed, we will be able to be disease free –able to get soundness of body.

If in any way…

In any way, if contrary existence or matter of bodily poison and of sick cells of the body is prepared– and made to enter the body, then bodily poison and sick cells or sick part of the cells will disappear or destroy. Then with new enthusiasm, the disease free body, refilling its shortage –due to wear and tear, will be able to get real and universal well-being through reformation. Being free from sickness expressing (disease) symptoms, mental symptoms– conduct-behaviors etc, everyone will be able to be well –strong bodied and minded human being.

The abstract of MahaPathic treatment procedure:

To cause to disappear –to destroy the disease-poison / toxin or the diseased bio-cells by just its contrary existence –is the fundamental thing of this system of treatment. At present, the treatment is done by the contrary existence of patient's disease-poison / toxin or sick-cells or urine, –collecting that material from patient's body, –the contrary existence is made by a secret procedure.

S-Existence and its Contrary Existence: Read the articl

**About the treatment of MahaPathy**

In this treatment, the selection of medicine is not of so problem, the main material of preparing the medicine is collected from the patient. Separate medicine for every patient –which is prepared only for that specified patient and applied only for that patient.

In case of difficult and chronic disease, where almost whole body and mind is attacked by poison of disease, usually in that case, medicine is prepared from patient's urine. The case in which poison of disease is confined within any organ or area, in that case, medicine is also prepared from sick cells of that area. Besides, in this treatment –medicines are also prepared from different type of abnormal discharges which are expressing sickness and in which may be the poison of diseases.

In case of chronic disease, when symptoms of disease are generally severe or acute, then only, it is proper time to collect urine or other abnormal discharge or secretion – for preparation of medicine. In maximum cases, in acute stage (of chronic disease) than latent stage, –the poison of disease is present more in patient's urine. But in very acute or serious stage, any abnormal discharge or urine should not be collected.

This treatment is simple –uncomplicated– but, medicine is prepared of high or higher influence –for a patient. So this treatment is expensive.

In this treatment, the role of the patient is also very important. Proper result receiving– depends on patient's proper following of the rules.

Except urine, discharge which is informing about sickness, as for instance– profuse saliva, pus, leucorrhea, mucus etc. also used for preparing the medicine.

In case of preparation of medicine from urine, another important thing is– in the first part of urine of the morning or dawn, in many cases, there is present prostate exudation or mucus and /or gonorrheal discharge, in which one or more of main disease-poisons or toxins are present.

One of the main causes of malnutrition is inability of our anabolic system and lack of digestibility. By use of 'MahaPathy' (–the new system of medicine), digestibility and anabolic ability come to the sound and normal state. In this way, MahaPathy is able to help us to make free from malnutrition and is able to make successful our 'Nutrients for All' program.

In case of nutrition, MahaPathic system of medicine takes an excellent part. MahaPathic medicine has an important role in covering the deficiency or losses of the materials (ingredients) of our body-cells. It incites the essential and nutritious materials of the body-cells which are draining away for any reason. As a result of that, the system of the body takes the initiative to recovery the losses gradually. Also MahaPathy medicine increases essential immunity of our body.

One thing we have to keep in our mind, always same poison or toxin does not produce the same symptoms in our body and mind. There may be produced various symptoms in our body according to our constitutions (The peculiar nature that which is formed on the base of our hereditarily obtained – make & materials, composition, distortion, ailments, toxins etc. and acquired defect & effects, diseases & toxins.) and the quantity of toxins

There may be produced different symptoms in different bodies except some similar symptoms, because of the presence of different sorts of toxins in different quantities. Everyday various sorts of poison or toxins are entering into our bodies in different quantities and making its inside and outside deformed and diseased gradually. Like a cross-bread people of various natures and appearances, our diseases also have become various sorts of natures.

One thing more, all systems of medicines are not fruitful for all diseases or problems. In some fields Herbal medicines are very effective, whereas in some other cases only allophonic medicines are capable to cure. Therefore if you are fond of any one system of medicine, then there is a chance to become unsuccessful in all cases. Whither the medicines are unable to react, there healing meditation, Yoga and different kind of psycho-spiritual or psychological healing methods can be useful. The best is –getting advice from a vast knowledgeable experienced person, to select first the system of treatment, that which would be right for the current or chronic problem.

An attractive thing is, medicine form– contrary impression of 'Super-Existence' (CISE) –after entering in our body and after being changed into 'Super-Existence' in the body, –if there is already present anything of opposite property, as there is performed the action of recovery in the way of 'MahaPathy', on the other side, –if there is already present anything harmful of similar property of the medicine (CISE), in our body, also in that case, the action of recovery is performed.

But, if there is present any bodiless 'Super-Existence' of similar property instead of anything (matter or element) of similar property, in that case, because of much amount of 'Super-Existence', there may be exposed the action of poisoning.

MahaPathic medicine and procedure of taking

In this treatment procedure patient's medicine is only one, –here it is no need to select and change a medicine. Only strength or subtlety of medicine needs to be changed. Still the procedure of preparing the medicine is kept secret.

In this treatment procedure, in very minute dose (amount) medicine is taken –in gradually increasing strength or subtlety. Gradually increasing the strength of medicine (or gradually making the medicine more subtle) by the doctor or manufacturer, –the responsibility is entrusted on the patient.

In this treatment procedure –liquid medicine is given in a glass-phial to the patient. Everyday in the morning, patent have to take ten drop of medicine from this phial of liquid medicine.

Nothing can be taken or drunk one hour before and after –taking the medicine. It is good to take medicine in empty stomach. Before taking medicine, the mouth –tongue teeth has to be brushed and washed with water only. In necessity, water can be drunk before taking medicine.

In the morning, to brush the teeth with toothpaste or toothpowder –is a general habit of many, but in this treatment, it is prohibited to use any type of peppermint, menthol, camphor food –drink and toothpaste or toothpowder. Besides this, neem (Azadirachta indica) or other twig (used as toothbrush) and tobacco –cannot be used.

Gradually if feeling relieved, as the patient proceeds towards cure– according to that, the medicine has to be taken at the interval of two days, later– at the interval of three days – gradually at one week interval. If the symptoms of disease increase (aggravate) after taking medicine, if a little or a little more increase, then as mentioned before medicine has to be taken at the interval of two to seven days, depending on intensity of aggravation. But if increases too much, the taking of medicine has to be stopped, while the aggravation of symptoms are present. After aggravation, if relief is seen, then also medicine has to be stopped. In some cases, suppressed disease or disease-symptoms can be reappeared. Also in these cases, medicine has to be stopped, while the symptoms are present.

If skin disease or eruption is seen, after taking of medicine, -no ointment should be used on that. If rheumatic pain increases– effort has to be made, to tolerate that. If it is intolerable, temporarily one or two allopathic pain killer tablets can be taken. But no steroid is allowed.

In some cases, after judging the patient's condition– on amelioration or aggravation of symptoms, taking of medicine is stopped. As long as the amelioration or symptoms of aggravation is present or will continue, till that time, the taking of medicine will be stopped.

Here a thing is worth mentioning, dropper, hand or any other object cannot be inserted into the medicine phial.

The lid of the phial has to be replaced immediately after the medicine is taken. The medicine phial has to be kept away from the direct heat or sun.

It is necessary to tell something, regarding the collection of main material of medicine. Besides, in this process– to be mentioned of some rules to be followed, for the collection of main material from patient's body, for the preparation of medicine.

The patient cannot take any medicine, customary empiric medicine, exciting food– drinks, addiction things –any drug or liquor, from fifteen days before, collection of patient's urine, for the preparation of medicine. From three days before, to, collection of urine, the patient has to take, only vegetable, boiled rice, handmade bread, milk (pure). It is prohibited to take salt or salty, sweet and bitter things, hot (chilly), sour, exciting food –drink, any drug or tobacco. Too much hard work, irregularity, over strain, awaking night etc cannot be done. The morning on which patient's urine will be collected, the previous night; patent must has to be without food.

On the specified date of urine taking– an ounce of urine has to be taken from the first urine of the morning, to be collected in the sterilized –purified bottle, supplied by the MahaPathy treatment center.

During the treatment period, the patient needs to follow some rules. It is prohibited, – taking any exciting food –drinks, any drug or addiction things, coffee, camphor peppermint mixed food or drinks, bitter and astringent food or drinks etc are prohibited.

Females need to stop taking medicine during monthly menstruation.

For brushing the teeth– toothpaste or toothpowder should not be used. Instead of that, one kind of white powder, supplied by the treatment center, can be used or only water- brush can be done.

During the period of treatment unsystematic lifestyle should not be followed. Patient should be free from impure – infectious intercourse.

After feeling the action (aggravation or amelioration) of medicine– it is duty to inform the doctor. Besides this, as per necessary, patient should contact doctor at interval of every fifteen days or one month. If there is much aggravation of the disease, then it should be understood that there has been some irregularity in taking of medicine, or the period of suffering from disease, is going to finish. That means cure or free from disease is approaching. Besides this, suppressed disease– especially rheumatic pain, skin disease etc may expose at many times. In that case, medicine taking should be stopped –contact should be made with the doctor and suggestion should be taken. The direction of getting cured from the disease is generally from inner to outer and top to bottom gradually.

If sufficient recovery or cure has been felt, the taking of medicine has to be stopped, as per the suggestion of the doctor. When medicine taking is stopped, closing the lid of the medicine phial –tightly, it is necessary to preserve that, by the help of the doctor, so that if needed in future, that can be used again, as per the suggestion of doctor.

In many cases, it may be necessary to use more high powerful medicine, twice or thrice. In that case, to make more high power medicine from this medicine, patient has to apply to the medicine manufacturer through the treatment centre. In future, if any disease seen, then if it is not cured by this medicine, in that case, again new medicine may be needed to prepare.

Along with taking this medicine– effort and arrangement to be made to be always happy –cheerful, and along with that, by practice of 'MahaYoga' procedures ('Maha-Sabasana', 'Maha-Yoga-Sleep' etc) –attainment of universal soundness is possible.

After taking the (high strength / influential) medicine (– given to the patient), if any action is not felt within one month, then it should be understood– more high strength or subtle medicine is necessary for that patent. In that case, more subtle or high influential medicine has to be prepared, as per the suggestion of the doctor.

Besides that, if the prevention and defense system is very weak or very excited and if the power of reaction of the body is lost– for serious sickness and/or taking many types of medicines, besides that in case of abnormal constitution, many times , after taking of medicine –patient may not feel any effect (action or reaction) of the medicine.

By this procedure of treatment, almost every disease can be treated, but its medicine preparation is time consuming and expensive, usually it is noticed to be used, for the treatment of serious and chronic diseases.

When any customary (current) procedure of treatment does not help to cure the disease, then the MahaPathy's astonishing efficacious excellence– greatness is felt. And for that reason– this is – MahaPathy.

Why the subtlety of medicine is increased gradually

If in the body, any poison is present in large or much amount, by this medicine (CISE), that poison cannot be made completely removed or make to disappear. Because, to remove that poison, the defense system of the body– much amount of 'CSE' of that poison has to be prepared from this medicine, which is beyond the capacity of the body.

When any poison enters the body in great amount– then the defence system of the body gets into disorder. Then the body cannot do the defence and remedial work systematically. Beside this, in form of medicine, that poison's CISE (from which –body prepares 'CSE') we get (in procedure of MahaPathic subtilization) less– more, in different subtle form. This subtle bodied 'CSE' is easily capable to remove or disappeared its similar formed subtle bodied contrary matter (poison), which is present in the body, at the (in more or less) old or chronic stage of the disease.

If anyone, after taking in great amount poison –takes the medicine (CISE) prepared from that poison, in that case, all the bodily poison cannot be removed by that medicine. By MahaPathic procedure, we cannot make contrary matter or any material contrary existence. If it is possible (in future) to prepare that, by any other procedure, then this problem –may not be there, then we will be able to remove or disappeared the great amount material poison, in the body.

Definitely in the case of old or chronic disease, also in case of new disease– the poison of the disease, is present in our body, in (–different level or degree) subtle bodied form. Generally, when the symptoms of disease are seen on body – mind, a little or long before that, the cells of the body have been started to be attacked. Till the cells are not attacked in some more amounts, we cannot feel any specific problem. Even if we feel a little, we do not care so much.

Between any poison and body cell, during action –reaction taking place –along with the passage of time, the bodily poison, gradually attains subtlety. Through this action –

reaction, in the poison and body cells– in both, more or less, changes take place.

It may not be that, the poison of the whole body, having equal subtlety. According to obtained (inner) environment – situation –happening, each poison particle may have separate states.

Any subtle bodied (the form of CISE) medicine –of any specific degree or potency –is able to remove or disappear the poison –properly, which is similar subtle –contrary-existence of that medicine. Also it is able to remove partly or sometimes wholly its nearest subtle bodied poison. But if there is great difference in the level or degree of subtlety, many times, both are unable to remove each other. For this reason, to remove or disappeared –the different formed subtle bodied poison; it is to take help of the similar subtle or gradual more subtle medicine-form 'CISE' –contrary impression of 'Super-Existence' of that poison.

In case of matter, the limit of subtleness is not extended to very far. But the limit of subtlety of 'CISE' is extended to a long distance. Though, all things have the end. The limit of subtlety of material poisons are not extended to a very long distance. However old, it is in the body.

Definitely in the case of old or chronic disease, also in case of new disease– the poison of the disease, is present in our body, in (–different level or degree) subtle bodied form. Generally, when the symptoms of disease are seen on body – mind, a little or long before that, the cells of the body have been started to be attacked. Till the cells are not attacked in some more amounts, we cannot feel any specific problem. Even if we feel a little, we do not care so much.

Between any poison and body cell, during action –reaction taking place –along with the passage of time, the bodily poison, gradually attains subtlety. Through this action – reaction, in the poison and body cells– in both, more or less, changes take place.

It may not be that, the poison of the whole body, having equal subtlety. According to obtained (inner) environment – situation –happening, each poison particle may have separate states.

Any subtle bodied (the form of CISE) medicine –of any specific degree or potency –is able to remove or disappear the poison –properly, which is similar subtle –contrary-existence of that medicine. Also it is able to remove partly or sometimes wholly its nearest subtle bodied poison. But if there is great difference in the level or degree of subtlety, many times, both are unable to remove each other. For this reason, to remove or disappeared –the different formed subtle bodied poison; it is to take help of the similar subtle or gradual more subtle medicine-form 'CISE' –contrary impression of 'Super-Existence' of that poison.

In case of matter, the limit of subtleness is not extended to very far. But the limit of subtlety of 'CISE' is extended to a long distance. Though, all things have the end. The limit of subtlety of material poisons are not extended to a very long distance. However old, it is in the body.

But, when a poison gets lost its individual form, bringing about deformity of body cells–, and after that, when that deformed cells do abnormal behavior like action of poisoning, continuously for a long time, as a result of that, one time, the nature– character etc of those sick cells– is included as a code –in the gene of the body. Then truly, that poison-existence is obtained a too subtle state.

In this case, not from the poison, –using the medicine (CISE) of extremely subtle form , prepared from that deformed sick cells, –it become possible to be free from serious disease in many respects or some time in all respects.

Why minute dose of the medicine is used

As the total amount of medicine-particle has the grossness and minuteness, similarly, every particle of the medicine has the bodily corpulence and subtlety. From this bodily corpulence to gradual subtlety, different stages are expressed in different gradually higher strength or subtle form. And, in amount, from grossness to different stages of gradual minuteness –these are gradually expressed in the form of gradual minute amount (dose).

If more quantity or amount of medicine (CISE) enters into the body, usually the body as per its capability – accepts very little part, and does the processing. But at various times, based on different physical conditions, different incidents may take place. Sometimes the body may refuse to accept in any part, and to do the processing of much quantity of medicine (as CISE). Again, sometimes may be, accepting and processing in much quantity– may call for its own danger.

If the amount of 'CSE' is created more, than amount of poison, present in the body, –disturbance –indiscipline – harm may take place– inside the body. Extra 'CSE' or contrary Super-Existence can lead to the causing of action of poisoning by oneself.

In the body, in minute amount– if increasing subtle medicine (CISE) enters, there is not to be afraid of so much of harm. And for any reason if harm is seen, stopping the medicine– easily that can be controlled.

# The scientific way to alleviate global poverty

The scientific way to alleviate global poverty

'MahaManan' self-development education is the scientific way to allheviate global poverty

Lack of sufficient knowledge and consciousness is the root cause of poverty.

By giving all kinds of facilities, and necessary help, to a poor man with a little knowledge and a little consciousness, maybe his/ her temporary poverty relief, but for a long time he will not be able to escape poverty.

If a rich man who has a lot of wealth, either hereditarily or otherwise, has a shortage of knowledge and consciousness, soon he could lose all his wealth and become poor, unless he accepts the advice of a wise person. However, it is important to have some knowledge in order to perform the tasks of the wise person.

One needs to have sufficient knowledge and consciousness to constantly make money and resources and protect them.

It is not that when economic development or economic freedom is achieved, human development also will be happen.

As economic development progresses, human life can be temporarily comfortable, human wealth and human civilization can be improved, in conventional education, people can become highly educated, but it will not develop the human mind. And if the conscious mind does not develop enough, people will lose all their wealth and fall into poverty again.

Human development means I understand the development of the human mind. Development of consciousness or conscious mind.

If the human mind does not develop, no matter how glamorous it looks, human beings will remain in the darkness in which they was.

Religious obstacles in the way of the spontaneous development of the human mind, the blindness, blind faith, and superstition that comes from ignorance, by removing these, if we can educate people in true mind-developmental basic education, if we can train them in mind-developmental practical procedure, then only human development will continue to develop.

If human (mind) development does not happen, all other development will be like pearl-garland in the monkey's neck. And if human development happens, then other areas will continue to develop.

The only way to alleviate poverty is to launch the 'MahaManan'' self-development curriculum extensively in all the countries which is performed by me. And at the same time, poverty can be eradicated if we can establish 'ManavDharma' in all.

'MahaManan' is an excellent incompatible system of essential basic education for true and universal self-development. It should be said here that the practical side of 'MahaDharma' religion is 'MahaManan' education.

This system of education removes ignorance, superstition and blind-faith from the human beings, and makes people aware and conscious as well as educates them in the essential basic education of life.

The root cause of poverty is blindness, superstition and blind-faith resulting from poor knowledge and low consciousness with physical and mental illness.

Not only free from poverty, human rights will be effective only when most people have enough knowledge and consciousness.

In addition, the scarcity of knowledge and consciousness are responsible for most human-caused problems, sickness and most awkward incidents.

The prevailing religion, politics, economics, administration, conventional education system, and any of the existing systems are not able to solve this problem.

To get rid of this extreme crisis,

Human-development-based religion~ 'MahaDharma' is the only way. This religion is not the same as conventional religion. This is a scientific method of true human development through an excellent and incompatible self-development education.

Our slogan is ~ 'मानवधर्म ही महाधर्म'

And, to make this epoch-making system reality, if most people come spontaneously, only then will real human development be possible with poverty alleviated.

An appeal to conscious people

We would like to make an acquaintance with an exceptional endeavor of human development and peace, through an excellent –incomparable system of essential education for true & universal self-development –world-wide.

'MahaManan' is an excellent – essential and fundamental education for true self-development and human development.

'MahaManan Kendra' is the education centre of that system of education. That is self-development or man making education centre.

We think, development of humankind or a nation is possible only through the development of individuals, also we think, customary or formal academic (school – college etc.) education is not sufficient for true development of human beings. For that, we need such an uncustomary (non-formal) basic human development education which can help us to be fully developed human beings.

It is known to every conscious person, the cause of most problems, poverty, – disturbances and crimes of human society –is the lack of true self-development education. Therefore the need of this education is undeniable.

At present, the demand of this essential education is found in conscious people. But there is no such institution for true self-development education in our country.

To make a better world –to make our life blessed –to fulfill oneself, to remove the inhuman activities and poverty from our society, we have an excellent – incomparable system of essential education for true & universal development.

The creator of this system of education is Maharshi MahaManas. We are desirous to establish the way of universal development of human beings –world-wide, and also we are desirous to establish a true and universal Human Development education center of international standard.

We need like-minded persons for our true Human Development program. If you are interested in this program, please extend your helping hands to make it possible.

To know more, please search: MahaManan, MahaDharma

Contact: WhatsApp: 9733999674

Please share this application as much as possible. Thank you.

# Can science be believed without hesitation

Science is true, this idea needs to change.

Like everything else science is also the apparent truth. What scientists are establishing as true today may be proven false tomorrow. Therefore, taking everything as the apparent truth is science.

For a long time, our favorite and respected "science" has been the victim of a conspiracy by a class of very greedy businessmen! 'Science' has been highly tainted, especially by a class of medicine or drug industrialist and traders. Part of this medicine trade continues to deceive us day after day.

Then there are the arms or war-weapon

dealers. They have enslaved science to their nefarious narrow interests. People are becoming helpless and oppressed by them.

The ultimate misuse of science is also happening in the field of information and digital technology. You say, science is not responsible for this!

In short, 'science' is the process of verifying theories, ideas and information through a systematic way, or analysis, and research, and the knowledge and results obtained from that research are also called science.

Now, the way people use this system and knowledge called science, it will produce results!

Science is not a matter of belief or disbelief. To believe in it means to believe in all the people who are working with it. Now, can all those people be trusted without hesitation!? No, they can't be trusted.

There are all kinds of people, good and bad, among scientists. There is greed, superstition, politics, manipulation, lobbying, hatred, honesty and dishonesty. There are many conspiracy victims, and conspirators.

Many people in the field of religion, science and politics are in fact very ordinary people, a judge whose verdict can turn many things upside down is also an ordinary person. s/he may also be a bigoted, superstitious man.

So, whatever scientists do or say, without judging enough in the name of science, without understanding it well, believing blindly is blind-faith. Scientists will always say right or true, this false idea is also blind-faith.

The same is true in the case of blind-faith in the scriptures and the words of the religious and political leaders. Blind faith is a firm belief, which cannot be shaken by any argument.

Science means true and tested. Science can be believed without hesitation, still be free from this blind idea. Telling people to be vigilant. Only after deep judgment and thorough verification can one accept the words of science and the results of science.

If we accept everything from them with blind faith, without understanding the advantages and disadvantages of science indiscriminately, if we accept the gift of science, we will finally be in a terrible predicament. Then there will be no time to sorry. This applies not only to science, but also to religion, politics, and the like. A very difficult time is ahead, so we must always be vigilant.

If we believe everything by closing our eyes or looking up on the surface, we will be in grave danger. I know that it will be a little difficult for the blind believers, who are blind fans or supporters of science as much as religion, to tolerate this accusation about science. Thank you.